Copyright © 2018 Clavis Publishing Inc., New York

Originally published as *Dapper Duimelijntje* in Belgium and Holland by Clavis Uitgeverij, Hasselt—Amsterdam, 2017
English translation from the Dutch by Clavis Publishing Inc., New York

Visit us on the Web at www.clavisbooks.com.

Brave Thumbelina written and illustrated by An Leysen

ISBN 978-1-60537-421-5

This book was printed in June 2018 at Publikum d.o.o., Slavka Rodica 6, Belgrade, Serbia.

First Edition
10 9 8 7 6 5 4 3 2 1

Clavis Publishing supports the First Amendment and celebrates the right to read.

An Leysen

BRAVE THUMBELINA

Clavis

NEW YORK

Once upon a time,

there was a young woman who lived in a beautiful house.
She had everything to be happy, but she was lonely.
More than anything she wanted a child.

One day, an old lady walked by her house. She stopped when she heard
the woman sighing. "What is it, dear?" she asked. "Why are you looking so sad?"
"Oh," the young woman answered. "I am so lonely! If only I had a child
to take care of. That is my biggest wish. But unfortunately, I can't have any children!"
"I can help you," the old lady said with a smile. She reached into her bag and
took out a little seed. "Put this seed in a flower pot with a lot of earth
and take good care of it."

The woman was very grateful, but also a bit confused. Why did the old lady give
her a flower seed when she'd asked for a child? She didn't know that the old lady
was in fact a witch. A good witch with magical powers. But with nothing else to do,
the young woman followed the instructions. She filled a pot with earth, planted the seed,
and took good care of it.

A few days later, the seed grew into a lovely flower.

The woman bent over to admire the flower.
Between the petals, she saw two little eyes looking up at her.

There was a tiny girl inside the flower!

The girl looked exactly like the child
the woman had been dreaming of.
She was beautiful.
But . . . she was not bigger than a thumb!

"My own sweet little *Thumbelina*,"
the woman sang while she lifted the girl carefully
with two hands and placed her to sit
on the edge of a teacup.

Thumbelina and her mother had a good life together.
The house was the perfect playground for the tiny girl.
She played among the dinnerware on the kitchen table.
She daydreamed atop the teacup.
She used a leaf to float from one side
of a soup bowl to the other.

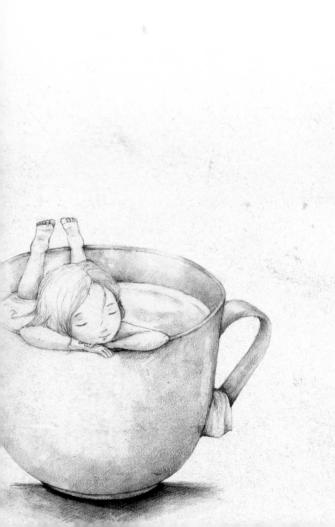

The woman made a soft bed of petals
for *Thumbelina* inside a box.
Every evening she sang a lullaby until *Thumbelina* fell asleep.
Then she carefully closed the box and placed
it safely next to her bed.

One spring evening, a big toad jumped through the open window.
She saw the box by the woman's bed and was curious.
She lifted the lid and peeked inside.
"What a beautiful bride for my son!" she croaked.
The toad carefully took *Thumbelina* out of the box
and carried her straight to the pond where her son lived.

The toad swam to a big lily pad, lay the sleeping *Thumbelina* down,
and brought her son to meet his bride. "CROAK, CRRROAK, CRRROAK" was all
he said when he saw the tiny girl.

Thumbelina woke up from the noise and saw two ugly toads
in front of her. She shuffled backwards on the lily pad in fear.
"Doesn't my son look handsome in his fancy suit?" the mother toad croaked
to *Thumbelina*. "You will be a perfect pair once you're married!"
And with that, she hopped away.

Thumbelina shuddered at the idea of marrying the toad, and burst
into tears. But the toad had no kind words for her. "CROAK, CRRROAK,
CRRROAK" was all he said before he vanished in the reed.

Thumbelina thought she was alone, but two little fish swam in the water beneath the lily pad. They saw what was happening and would not let this poor little girl spend her life with the thoughtless, horrible toads! So they began to chew on the stem of the lily pad until it broke.

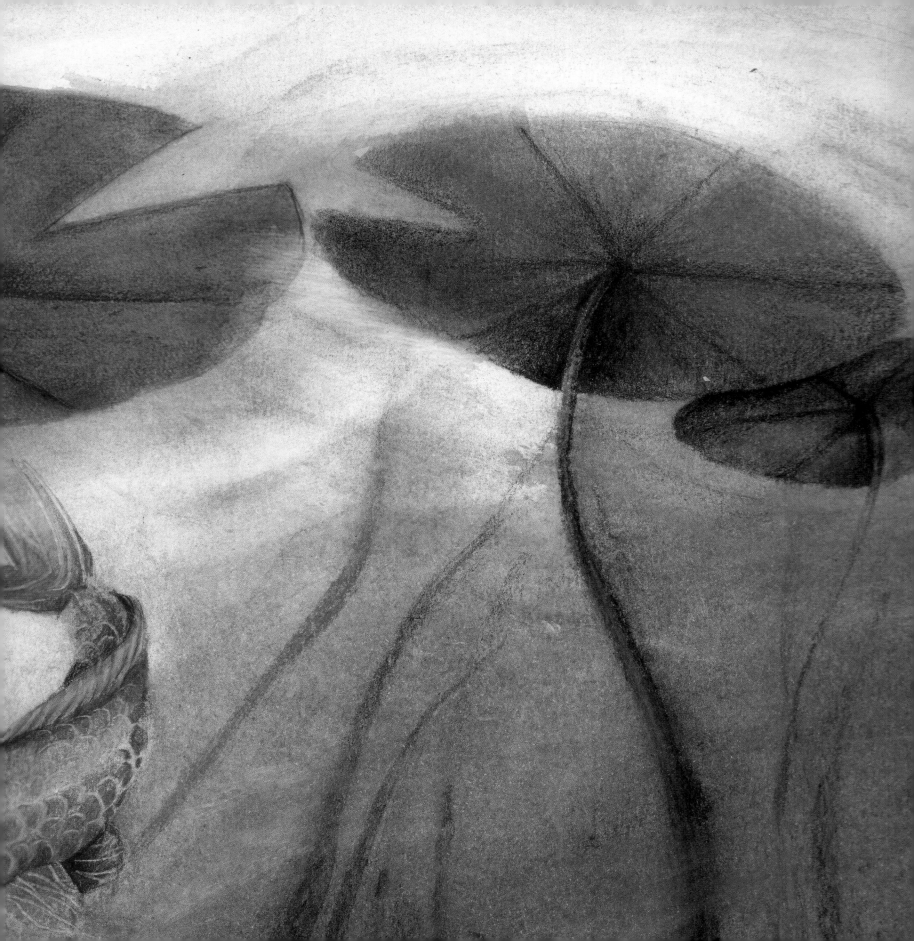

Thumbelina floated on her lily pad, farther and farther away from the toads. The sun was shining bright and the water was sparkling in its golden light. The air was filled with the sound of happy, twittering birds that flew around the pond and whistled to one another. *Thumbelina* felt relieved, but she could not float here forever. She saw a butterfly fluttering by and quickly loosened her hair ribbon. She tied one end around the little body of the butterfly while she firmly grabbed the other end. The butterfly lifted her high in the sky.

How wonderful to soar through the air, thought *Thumbelina*.
Then, out of the blue, a big june bug flew by.
When he saw *Thumbelina*, he wanted her all to himself.
He pulled her roughly from the butterfly and carried her
to the top of a beech tree.

He wanted to show her off to all the other june bugs.
But the other june bugs did not share his admiration for *Thumbelina*.
They found her plain and unattractive.
So the june bug lost interest in *Thumbelina* and flew away.

Alone again, *Thumbelina* slipped out of the tree and landed in the soft high grass. What a relief. She'd escaped from that pushy june bug!

Thumbelina began to wander and soon she came to a clearing in the woods. She immediately felt at home. She weaved a bed of grass and hung it under a fern leaf. It kept her dry when it was raining. *Thumbelina* ate berries and nuts and delicious sweet honey. And when she was thirsty, she drank the dew drops that lay on the petals every morning.

Summer quickly passed. As autumn winds began to blow,
the birds that whistled such nice songs for *Thumbelina*
all left for warm countries. The trees lost their leaves
and the plants lost their flowers. The big fern leaf where
Thumbelina had lived for so long shriveled
until there was nothing left but a faded yellow stem.

Thumbelina felt terribly cold.
She wrapped herself in a dry leaf to get
a little warmth, but it did not help.

Winter came and it started to snow. Thumbelina knew she had
to find a warm hiding place. The icy winter wind blew the brave girl
forward, until she came to a house made of dry twigs.
A little frightened, Thumbelina knocked on the door.
A mouse curiously stretched out her nose. When she saw the girl
standing there, chilled to the bone and shaking, she took pity on her.

"Poor thing," the mouse peeped. "Come in!"
The cottage was small and cozy—there were
shelves and cupboards full of all kinds of things,
and jars and bowls of food. "You can stay here
during winter," the mouse said, and she pointed
around. "There's more than enough for the two
of us." And so *Thumbelina* moved into the
mouse's home and they began to spend the cold
winter together.

One evening there was a loud pounding on the door.
"Oh! That must be my neighbor," the mouse exclaimed.
"He's so wealthy and handsome! He lives in a big house
with hallways and corridors. And he has such fancy clothes.
Oh, *Thumbelina*, if you would marry him, you would
never be cold again. But . . . he's blind. You will have to tell him
the most beautiful stories you know. Then he will like you just
as much as I do."
The mouse opened her door and the mole swung into the room.
Thumbelina immediately disliked him. He might be rich and
well educated, but he spent all of his time in the coolness of his
cave deep under the ground. He didn't care for the warmth
of the sun, the flowers, the birds and the bees.
But the mole immediately fell in love with
Thumbelina! He was drawn toward
her bright voice when she told him stories and
sang him a song.

The mole invited *Thumbelina* and the mouse to visit
his home. With some dry twigs he made a fire that lit up
the dark corridors. He guided his guests through his vast home.
Suddenly they collided with a swallow lying down on the ground.
Thumbelina and the mouse were startled and stepped back.
But the mole only kicked the bird with his short legs.
"I'm glad I am not a bird who can only twitter in summer
and starves in winter," he scolded, and he walked
on as if nothing had happened.

That night *Thumbelina* could not sleep. She thought of that poor swallow over and over again. She sneaked into Mole's home and gently covered the swallow with her own blanket.

Then she bent and gently kissed him on his closed eyes.
"Goodbye, sweet bird," she whispered, gliding her head against his chest.
But then *Thumbelina* heard something . . .

The bird's heart was beating! The swallow was not dead.
He was only still from the cold. *Thumbelina* shivered.
She felt sorry for the poor bird and took care of him as best
as she could. Every day she returned to bring him water and
some grains. The swallow hid in the dark hallway all winter long.
And the mole and mouse knew nothing about it.

Time passed and the snow melted under the spring sun.
It even warmed the swallow under the ground. Soon he was
ready to spread his wings again. "Come with me," he said many
times. But *Thumbelina* did not want to disappoint the mouse.
She said goodbye to her good friend and waved at him until
he disappeared at the horizon.

"Oh, *Thumbelina*. You're so lucky!" the mouse peeped, excited,
when the mole finally proposed to *Thumbelina*. He brought her the finest
lace and she set about to make a wedding dress. The mole visited her every
night to see how she was doing. At the end of summer, they would have
a perfect wedding!

But *Thumbelina* was not happy, not even a bit. She did not care
for the mole, and the idea of living her life underground made her cry.
"Rubbish!" the mouse said. "The mole is a very suitable husband for you.
With his handsome clothes and a house as big as a palace.
You should be grateful!"

The big day dawned and the mole came for *Thumbelina*
to live underground with him. Now she would never feel
the hot sunshine ever again . . .

She was allowed to go outside one last time to say goodbye
to the green forest and the flowers and the birds. Tears
flowed from her eyes when suddenly . . . TWEET, TWEET!
Thumbelina immediately recognized the sound. It was
her good friend the swallow. He flew right over her head.
"*Thumbelina*," he sang. "Winter is coming.
I'm going to a country far away where it is summer
all year long. Join me. I can carry you on my back."
This time *Thumbelina* did not hesitate. She jumped
on the bird's back and held on to him tightly.

The swallow flew higher and higher,
over woods, over seas, and over mountains
covered with snow. When *Thumbelina*
got chilly, she nestled into her friend's feathers.
Only her head peeked outside to see
the wonderful world beneath her.
The farther they flew, the more impressive
the landscape became. The swallow finally
settled down on the most beautiful
place *Thumbelina* had ever seen.

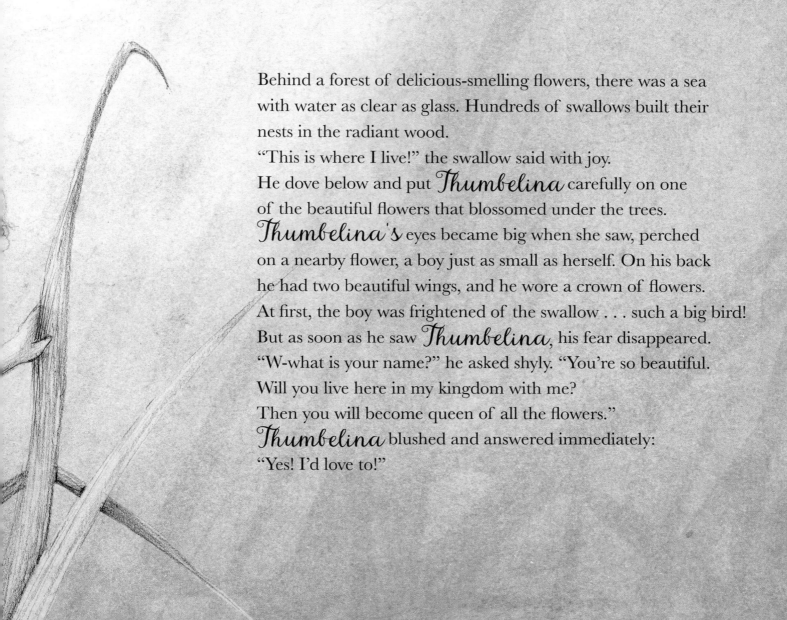

Behind a forest of delicious-smelling flowers, there was a sea with water as clear as glass. Hundreds of swallows built their nests in the radiant wood.

"This is where I live!" the swallow said with joy.

He dove below and put *Thumbelina* carefully on one of the beautiful flowers that blossomed under the trees. *Thumbelina's* eyes became big when she saw, perched on a nearby flower, a boy just as small as herself. On his back he had two beautiful wings, and he wore a crown of flowers.

At first, the boy was frightened of the swallow . . . such a big bird! But as soon as he saw *Thumbelina*, his fear disappeared.

"W-what is your name?" he asked shyly. "You're so beautiful. Will you live here in my kingdom with me?

Then you will become queen of all the flowers."

Thumbelina blushed and answered immediately:

"Yes! I'd love to!"

With her prince, *Thumbelina* could live a life under the sun.
She didn't have to fear a life in a cold pond in the company
of an ugly toad or deep under the ground with a spoiled mole.
Thumbelina couldn't believe that she could be so happy.
And if that wasn't enough, the flower prince gave her wings.

Now she was free to go wherever she liked.

And the very first thing the happy couple did
was return to visit her mother,
who had been so kind to her.